AUTHO
SKETCH AR~~TIST: JESSE ~~~~~~

HARBOR
YARNS

outskirts
press

PROMOTIONAL BLURBS

"Reminiscent of Tristan Jones, *Harbor Yarns* is a delightful collection of short stories you might hear around a campfire or over a few beers at the boatyard. Some might not be true, some might be exaggerated, but you'll quickly not care as you enjoy these tales from a born storyteller."

—Lanna Waterman, retired public schoolteacher and chairperson of the Olean, New York, library board

"When I'm not flinging lines into still or running water, I'm looking for good reading about such a world and watery ways. Gary Larson's *Harbor Yarns* does that and more, taking me to a waterfront village whose inhabitants drew their livelihood from the big water close by. Here is a stringer full of tales about simple but colorful fisherfolk and fishmongers; of adventures in rowboats, canoes, and sailing ships; tales of human foibles, as well as accounts of travelers passing through, all touched by the town of Little Cove. Savor 'em a bite at a time, and rejoice!"

—Angus Watkins, author of *Gathered at the River*

"Gary Larson's *Harbor Yarns* takes the reader on a delightful romp back to the old fishing haunt of Little Cove, and its ever-present gathering of 'smelly fishermen, scallywags, drunks, and liars.' The characters that Larson details are interesting, amusing, outlandish, wacky, and insane, but always fun. His yarns will leave you feeling like you've had a bite taken out of you by a sea serpent, much like the land for which Little Cove was named, and will hook you right down to your very innards. His book is a good catch."

—Chuck Pora, contributing writer for the *Erie Times-News* and author of seven books

ACKNOWLEDGMENTS

First and foremost, I thank my wife, Sarah, for her fifty years of companionship and for her helpful dialogue for this book. I also thank my family and friends who offered unconditional encouragement and valued guidance. I thank the many people who read various chapters and urged me to "write on." Next to thank are my editors, Dean Baldwin, professor emeritus of English, Penn State Behrend, and Eugene H. Ware, author of several books on Erie, Pennsylvania's Presque Isle and three lighthouses.

1

A FINE SPIT, MOSTLY

YEARS AGO, ON a great lake, on the southern shore, a little cove was named just that: "Little Cove." No one can remember who named it or when, but it seemed to fit. As is this lake's way, it formed this spit of land because of a strong westerly wind. Over the centuries, wave action from west winds pushed sand to the east and created this cove, peninsulas, and even islands. But, many years ago, the early residents of Little Cove didn't understand this science. They thought the cove looked as if a giant sea monster had taken a bite out of the shore.

The cove was adequate though certainly not an ideal natural harbor. Nevertheless, fishermen arrived in small numbers and then more as the years rolled on. They say the lake then was so abundant with fish that one could literally catch them using buckets. There were pike, sturgeon, white fish, bass, catfish, and dozens of other species. The fish were caught, cleaned, dried or packed in ice, and then hauled by horse and wagon to three neighboring villages. There they were marketed to broader locations. It may be fact or it may be legend that millions of pounds of fish were harvested from the great lake.

Many different fishing boats harbored tightly in Little Cove over the years. Fishermen plied their trade in small, open, wooden rowboats and sailboats, and later in enclosed metal boats that looked more like submarines than anything friendly.

The cove did its best to protect the residents from southeast through west to northwest blows. But squalls or storms from the north and northeast were feared by all. It's not only on the oceans that the great nor'easter comes to call in the early spring and late autumn. Waves twelve to fifteen feet tall could rip the boats off their moorings, tossing them in shore a hundred yards. Wind is formidable. Water and wind are majestic powers to behold!

"It's dark as pitch out there," one old fisherman bemoaned. "If we get back after sundown, why, we can hardly see Little Cove."

Indeed, on the lake at night, the shore could look the same as the water. The best-eyed sailors couldn't see the rocks. To help, a cylinder lighthouse and a keeper's house were erected with local stone. An unusual energy was used to light it. Natural gas was discovered nearby in a stone well. It was channeled underground through hollow wooden logs and up to the top of the tower, where the gas light was lit. Many a sailor and fisherman found his way back to Little Cove thanks to that beacon of hope and the faithful lighthouse keepers.

But, as years passed, the lake wielded its destructive force. Storms took their toll on moored fishing boats and docks, so locals conceived break walls for protection.

"We have to do it, or our boats will be washed away someday."

A V-shaped design was penciled. Two walls would be built from land at an angle, nearly coming together out in the lake. The narrow opening would be the access to the lake. The inside walls would create a protected bay. Work began, but it was a huge project. It took years to cart tons of rock to build the walls.

"That'll keep those northeast waves from a-crashing in."

"Will it keep the great sea monster out?" Luke asked timidly.

"Oh, that's codswallop to be sure. There 'tain't no thing."

"That's what you say. I've heard otherwise. Fritz said he saw it out there. There's a creature swimmin' in that water, to be sure."

"Well, if there is, no little wall is going to keep us safe!"

"It never was built right," many a fisherman complained. "The lake's too strong. There's no wash through. It'll fill up with silt in a few years."

Fill up it did. Inside the northeast wall it was ten feet deep, and in just a few years, there was land where water should have been. Grass began to grow. After too many belts of rye whiskey, Jeremiah blurted out, "We'll be grazin' the goats in the harbor a-fore long." "Har, har," the fishermen bellered. Not until Little Cove filled in nearly halfway across did the dredging begin. But the fix was short lived. Again and again Little Cove filled in. Adequate depth for boats became more of a problem.

Only once, the old timers say, was the wall breached. It was when one of those megastorms took shape.

Angus, taking a long draw on his pipe, recollected, "It wasn't a nor'easter that came calling, but a nor'wester to everyone's surprise. A mighty December storm came rolling in, crashing fifteen-foot waves into the western break wall, shooting water into the air a hundred feet high. She kept a-banging into that wall, hour after hour. Then breach she did. The waves pushed a whole section about halfway out into Little Cove's harbor. It took us years to clean up."

During those years, Little Cove was less a safe harbor. But finally the wall stood again. Still, the townsfolk were pretty jittery wondering just what would happen next in Little Cove.

In the tavern one night, Sylvester kept twisting his mug round and round. Others observed, but no one spoke.

Then Sylvester announced, "I'm going down to the lake to take a little row in my boat."

Off he went. Nobody thought a thing about it. In the

morning, there on the shore was Sylvester's rowboat, but Sylvester was nowhere to be found. He wasn't home. He wasn't out fishing. He was gone.

Not until day's end did the topic come up again.

"He ain't nowhere to be seen."

"Where in hell is he?"

"His boat looks fit."

"The oars are still in it."

As the weeks went by, they looked for Sylvester's body to wash up. Nothing. There was not one shred of clothing—not a hat or a boot—nor rotten flesh to prove that Sylvester ever existed.

Some weeks later, deep in a game of poker one night at the tavern, Zeke blurted out, "Ya know, seems like ol' Sylvester was just ate up by a great sea monster. One bite and that was that."

A few sighed and nodded as Matty dealt a new hand.

2

LITTLE FREDDY FERGUSON

ROWING A BOAT requires that one face the rear or stern of the rowboat. With an oar in each hand, the oar blades are slipped into the water. With an even pull on each oar, the boat moves straight forward. Pulling on only one oar results in the boat going around in circles.

"Pullin' on one oar" became a derogatory phrase to describe a fisherman who was thought to be too stupid to know how to row a boat.

Mark Twain used another phrase, in reference to some others, that "there weren't enough brains among the lot to bait a fish hook."

Fishermen were thought to be stupid. Maybe they were. Maybe they weren't. They were smart enough to understand that their work was dangerous. They understood that leaving in the morning didn't guarantee that they would return in the evening. There was danger everywhere.

Some time ago, on one early morning, thick fog covered both harbor and home in Little Cove. Lanterns were lifted high as the men sleepily made their way to their boats, which were pulled far up onto shore. There were several dozen men in as many boats with their provisions for the day. For each there was a chunk of salted pork, fish, and hardtack. Drinking water came from the lake. No one took whiskey, tobacco, or a pipe. Those blessings would be enjoyed at day's end.

Thompson led, as his was the only boat with a compass. Mainsails were raised to catch the offshore breeze. Through the channel opening, the boats stayed as close as possible. The men peered through the fog to keep each other in sight.

Mackerel skies promised rain by late day. They had all agreed on the day's course and destination: north by northwest, three miles out to ten fathoms of water. Jibs went up. Thompson blew a blast on the horn every minute or so, as they would soon be out of sight with each other. The longer the boat, the faster she sailed. The vessels that left the harbor in a close fleet spread out like a fan into the beckoning lake.

Each man had a blow horn knowing well the signals. He sent one blast each minute in fog. Two short blows acknowledged they were still in range with the lead boat. Two longs, then a short meant Thompson had reached the destination. A short, then two longs meant someone was onto a school of fish. Four short blasts, a pause, and then four more short blasts meant distress; assistance was needed. But no fisherman in Little Cove would call for help, unless maybe for a broken bone.

Anchors were played out. Little scope was needed as the winds were still light. Some men were setting nets. Others were using hand lines with hooks. A dozen hooks at various depths increased the odds. On the best days, one could expect fish on every pull. The fish guts from the previous day's catch served as chum and bait. But there were many days when the fish weren't biting. Even the nets proved a futile effort.

It was well into the morning, and the summer's sun still struggled to burn off the fog. There was a chill. Then, like a sweep of the Almighty's hand, the fog lifted. It was gone. It became hotter than Hades in no time.

Each fisherman minded his own fishing boat but looked around to eye where the others were. Bill, Lazy Larry, Chuck,

Big Jim, and Trapper were a little in, closer to shore. Some of the boys were west a mite. Some went east. A few were farther north. But all were within sight of each other. Somehow, there was a security in that. Just knowing that the others were around was a comfort, especially if help was needed.

The fellas to the west seemed to be on the best school. Each had sounded a short and two long blasts.

By late afternoon, the clouds began to roll in. The blue sky became thick and dark. Each fisherman had a slicker, but no one would bother with it. They all looked forward to being cooled off by the rain. Slickers and boots were for early spring and late fall when rain turned to sleet, often hail. Being chilled to the core was a daily event.

A half-dozen boats weighed anchor. They reset near Freddy Ferguson. It wasn't the first time they would have their fun. Freddy always thought the others worked their way toward him because he was on the best school of fish.

"How's the fishin', Freddy?"

"Oh good, real good. How 'bout you fellas? Ya catching some?"

"Oh yeah, Freddy. If you can guess how many fish I have in my basket, I'll give you both of them."

"Har, har, har," the men would laugh.

"So, you got two and then some," Freddy would say.

"And then some, Freddy."

"Hey, Freddy, seen any of them flying fish today?"

"Oh, fellas, you know there ain't none."

Just about then, Whitey would reach down and grab a small carp. He'd fling it over toward Freddy's boat, and it would land in the water just a few feet away. "There's one, Freddy."

Freddy would look down at the splash, up to the sky, and then back down to the splash. He'd rub his head, then his chin.

"Fellas, I think I just saw one, one of them flying fish."

"You don't say, Freddy. We told you they was out here."

Freddy would shake his head, scratch his chin, and look here and there. The surrounding fishermen would start hurling carp toward Freddy's boat, always where he wasn't looking.

"There's one, Freddy. There's another one. There's another one."

Freddy would spin around trying to catch a glimpse of the fish.

"They're the ones with the wings, Freddy, the ones that fly just like a bird."

Freddy would spin around this way and that way. The fish would be splashing, but Freddy never had sense enough to look at the guys who were tossing them. Back and forth he'd go. He'd spin in circles, trying to get a good look at the flying fish, until he'd get so dizzy that he would fall face-first into his boat. The laughter went up with a roar.

"What a great joke on Freddy," the men would whisper to each other back at the tavern in Little Cove. The best part of it? They played the joke a hundred times, and Freddy never caught on. He always believed.

When they were back at the tavern, the men continued their fun, spinning yarns about the wild prairie "jack-a-lope," a rabbit with antlers. Of course, all of the men testified they'd seen one or two, everyone but Freddy. But he believed in the jack-a-lope too, just 'cause the fellas said so.

Freddy wasn't the only fool among the fishermen. They all had been on the short end of tricks. Given the right lie, the brightest of the lot could be a target for payback, a sucker for a scheme.

The day was ending back on the water. Ding-ding, ding-ding, ding-ding. Thompson rang his boat's bell. It was time to call it a day. Ten hours of fishing was long enough. There'd be more fish to catch tomorrow.

Thompson determined when to end the day's fishing by the size of the catch in the bottom of his boat. Sometimes the fish would cover the floorboards. Other times, there would not be one to bring back. But when they did catch fish, the work would begin for the women in Little Cove. Their job was to scale, gut, salt, and then dry or ice each of the day's catch. Sometimes the cleaning of fish would occupy the women into the wee hours of the morning.

So, a bit before day's end, anchors were weighed and sails raised. Whatever puff of wind was left in the day would take them back again to the harbor.

"We need to get back, Freddy, and soon."

"Why's that, Thompson?"

"Well, you remember ol' Sylvester, don't you?"

Well, Freddy did. He was there when they looked for Sylvester. They found nothing, not one thing. Sylvester was gone. Freddie knew what took him. He knew that Sylvester was supper for that great water beast. He didn't want to go that way. Freddie thought he was too young to die. When he did die, he wanted to pass in his own bed. He didn't want to be eaten up the way Sylvester was.

Freddy would often sail back on his knees. The men could hear him talking as if to himself. They could faintly hear his words: "Dear Father in heaven, bring me safe to Little Cove. Don't let me get ate up by no great sea monster."

None of the men would make fun of Freddy on the sail back home.

3

WOFFLEY, SADIE, AND SALLY

MALTHUS CLARENCE WOFFLEY was born in Wales, or so they say. How he got to Little Cove, nobody knows. He was not a fisherman. He wasn't suited to the work. He was a landlubber. He was a drunk's drunk. Malthus was everybody's joker, always ready for "one for the road, then another." Yet even he was needed in Little Cove. The men found a job suited to his talents.

He could drive a wagon. He did have a way with horses. He talked in their ears, and the horses' eyes would bulge as if they understood. "Gee" and "haw" were elementary commands to Malthus. He had in his repertoire a dozen words his horses seemed to know because they obeyed them. Fast, slow, trot, stop, eat, crap. They were as disciplined a team as any had ever seen. Sally and Sadie were their names.

Every other day it was Malthus's task to transport barrels of fish packed in ice to three neighboring villages: Bolt Corners, Cold Spring, and White Birch. From these villages the fish were sold to venders in other areas. The days Malthus drove the wagon were the high and holy days of his week. He looked forward to work. No one ever knew what he did on the off days, but he was always there on workdays.

The respective villagers were eager to receive the fish. The price per barrel had been agreed upon, so paying the bill was never an issue.

His route was a circle of sorts. First, he drove about six miles out to Bolt Corners, then another eight miles to Cold Spring, another six to White Birch, and nine miles or so back to Little Cove. He arrived at dawn in Little Cove with Sally, Sadie, and his wagon. It took only minutes to fill the wagon with barrels of fish, and then off he went.

He never packed a rifle. He never carried a lunch. He never took along a rain slicker. It was just Malthus, Sally, Sadie, and his wagon with barrels of fish. There was one more thing—his faithful companion, a friend he always had with him: one fine jug of rye whiskey.

Malthus Clarence Woffley would barely be out of sight from town before he took his first gulp.

"Argh, that be good rye today. Right fine rye. Maybe the best to ever cross me lips and hit me belly. You and I, friend, are going to get to know each other real well today."

So his day was a drinking day from before sunup until after sundown.

He was able to transact business on the first two stops, deliver the fish, and receive the pay. But by the time he hit White Birch, he was sloppy drunk. No matter, sober or not, he always dropped the pay in a wooden box under the seat. He was sure to close the lid. As he left White Birch, the locals would shake their heads wondering how long it would be before he'd pass out. No one was totally sure when that did happen. But pass out he did. The horses kept walking.

Back in Little Cove, in the predawn morning, there his wagon sat, stopped squarely at the shoreline. The horses would walk as far as the water's edge to slake their thirst with lake water. They'd just be there, standing. Malthus would be dead drunk, lying in the back of the wagon. The jug of rye was completely gone. The boys would unload the empty barrels.

They'd take the money from the box and turn the team around. With a slap on their asses, Sally and Sadie would be off to the barn, with Malthus bumping around in the back of the wagon.

Malthus would wake up at some point. God knows when. Stumbling to his bed, he'd sleep most of the day. For many years Sally and Sadie would take Malthus home. He was never quite sure how he got there. He was surely not going to ask.

4

THE SEASON OF MUSIC

THERE WAS A time, in late March, when a couple showed up in Little Cove with a push cart, common in those days. The push cart was large enough to carry all their life's possessions. It was, in fact, their home. They asked if they might spend a day or two camped by the shore. As they looked the type who would cause little trouble, they were given the nod. So it was.

Not long after setting up camp, they pulled out some instruments. Both started singing. Their music included ballads, sea shanties, and poems set to melody. The fishermen would stop to listen to a song but then move on. There wasn't much time for idleness in Little Cove.

The couple asked if they might move their cart under a roofed shelter that was built near the shore, a gathering spot in the warmer months with a few tables and chairs scattered around. Before long they had their belongings all over the place. Pots, pans, cups, and food lay all around. Laundry was hung on lines strung from post to post. Instruments were laid out for all to behold, the likes of which had never been seen in Little Cove.

Some of the folks in Little Cove recognized their violin. This couple could make it scream, then cry, and then give off tones so sweet the birds began to join them in their songs.

There was a whole array of other music makers. Something called a stringed dulcimer and another, a hammer dulcimer, apparently were related to Scottish bagpipes, though entirely different in appearance. There were flutes and horns of various sizes and shapes, one more unusual than the next. There was a drum, a tambourine, hitting sticks, and clappers. They knew how to play them all.

The couple would just look at each other and start to play and sing as if they had a script prepared beforehand. Especially after a day's fishing, after supper, folks would gather under the shelter. The couple would start right in with their music. They'd go from one song to the next and the next and the next, with just enough pause to take in some air.

> In Little Cove, a man did roam,
> No cabin had he to call his home.
> A sprightly chap of twenty-two,
> A shirt of green and pants of blue.
>
> His fate was like so many more,
> Until he met a tempting whore.
> Said she, "Come see me when you can."
> This sprightly chap, he should have run.
>
> But a man simply being a simple man,
> Who couldn't remember how it began,
> Went into her room for a closer look,
> And left in the morning as poor as a rook.

How the men of Little Cove smiled at that one. Each looked to the other as if to say, "That one was about me, you know." When this duo wasn't singing, it was spinning yarns. They told one about the MacLeod clan, pronounced "McCloud." The man began the story.

"Gavin and Jessie MacLeod immigrated to the United

States from County Loch Lomond, Scotland, or so they say. They settled and then opened a general store. Scots being Scots, they made money fast. Soon the children came, one after the other. First there was William, then Bruce, Robert, and finally Duff, four strapping boys.

"Duff wasn't his Christian name. But it was the only name folks knew him by from his birth to his death. It seems Duff was born old. He walked like an old man. He talked like an old man. He dressed like an old man. He was an old man when he was an old man. He was an old man when he was six years old. He was simply an 'old duffer.' Duff told us about his family as we passed through his town just a short time ago."

The man continued in Duff's raspy voice, "I guess we weren't the usual kind of family. We were always fighting, from the time we were young. All the way along, we fought. I don't mean yelling words. I mean fistfighting down in the dirt.

"Someone would say something. Off we'd go, punching and hitting until we wore ourselves out. Father and the four of us boys would all be rolling around, pulling ears, clawing at flesh. I don't know why, but we were always fighting. Over what? I don't know. We just fought all the time. Me poor Mum! She'd just stand to the side shaking her head.

"One time Bruce got beat up pretty bad, and though he really didn't know which of us was the cause, he figured it had to be Father. So, late one night, he came barging into the house, all drunk like a skunk. He did give Father the courtesy of a tongue-lashing first, before he effected his plan.

"'You no good bastard. You cod wallop, broken bum. You dung-filled bag of no good. You pile of tripe, fish guts, and cow shit. Now you're going to get yours.'

"He raised his shotgun and fired at Father. He hit him too. He hit him right in the neck, and then he stumbled out the door. Father fell to the ground. We were sure he was a goner. Blood was on the floor. Father was rolling here and there in pain. Somehow we got him settled down. We sewed him up as best we could. The shot tore a big chunk right out of Father's neck, but by some miracle of heaven, it didn't hit the jugular. It took some time for him to heal up. He always had that chunk of flesh missing from his neck. Father always wore a high-collared shirt from then on."

> Father MacLeod ran the general store.
> When fights began, he wanted more.
> Ruled the roost, didn't give a heck
> Till the middle boy put a bullet through his neck!

"Where'd ya learn all these songs there, mister?"

"We're minstrels, you know. We travel from this place to that. Everywhere we go, folks have some song to sing."

Loki piped up, "In the same way we pick up songs from the sailors who come by?

"That's right."

Loki continued, "The immigrants come through. Germans, Swedes, Irish—they're all heading west through the lakes or overland and then on. They stop here for our fish. We trade for supplies we wouldn't have otherwise. That's how we gets our whiskey, our salt, ropes, hooks, and bullets. The sailors like to sing. Shanties, I thinks they call them."

> Louis was the king of France
> Before the revolution.
> Away, haul away; we'll haul away, Joe.
>
> But then he got his head chopped off,
> Which spoiled his constitution.
> Away, haul away; we'll haul away, Joe.
>
> Once I was in Ireland
> Digging turf and praties,
> And now I'm on a Yankee ship

Hauling on sheets and braces.

Now when I was a little boy,
And so me mother told me
That if I didn't kiss the girls,
Me lips would all grow moldy.

Way haul away,
We'll haul away the bowline.
Way, haul away,
The packet is a rollin'.

"Why that's a good one," the couple complimented those who joined in the singing. "Do you know any more?"

"Oh, yes sir, we does. We've learned a lot over the years. When we're out there fishing all day, it's a grand way to pass the time. We even make some up as we go to fit our trade. This one is a good fit to sing whether yer raising sails or pullin' up nets."

Did you ever see a wild goose
Sailin' o'er the ocean?
Ranzo, ranzo, weigh heigh!

They're just like them pretty girls
When they gets the notion.
Ranzo, ranzo, weigh heigh!

The other mornin'
I was walkin' by the river
When I saw a young girl walkin'
With her topsails all a quiver.
I said, "Pretty fair maid,
and how are you this morning?"
She said, "None the better
For the seeing of you."

Did you ever see a wild goose
Sailin' o'er the ocean?
They're just like them pretty girls
When they gets the notion.

Sometimes when they weren't singing words, the two minstrels would just play their strings, tap the drum, and blow
their flutes or horns. Songs without words. Songs waiting for
words. Just the dance of sound beneath the evening stars.

"Sing the rat song, would ya?"

"You mean the 'Two Little Rodents'?"

"Yar, that be the one. Sing on."

Two little rodents floating on a raft.
One was forward, one was aft.
One had blue eyes, one had green.
The lovesickest rodents you've ever seen.
Dance, boatman, dance.

Off they sailed to a land far away,
Where warm breezes blow and palm trees sway.
Sailed away on the old gulf stream.
Warm days, cool nights, living life like a dream.
Dance, boatman, dance.

"Then there's that one about the old fat boat, kind of like
my boat, the *Gypsy Gal*. You know that one, don't ya, girl?
Sing that one about the old fat boat."

Got an old fat boat.
She's slow, but she's handsome.
Hard in the chime and soft in the transom.
I love her and she loves me,
But I think it's just for my money.

"Ah, that's a good one," Angus mused. "It might go well with the bagpipes. Oh God, I miss the pipes of Edinburgh. How did I end up in this place? I miss me home. I surely do. It makes a man wonder how he gets to where he got."

The spring slipped into summer, the summer into fall. There was a different sort of feel to Little Cove with those players around. It seemed like there was less fightin'. The fellers weren't as testy. The women breathed more deeply. Who's to know what spell these two may have cast?

Maybe their favorite song of all was the one learned by all the folks from Little Cove. The minstrels would sing it again and again. It was an easy enough song. The melody was soft; there was sweetness to it.

> Fill up your glasses
> With good ol' lager beer.
> "We're a long time dead," the wise man said,
> "So have a good time here."
>
> We'll drink to the health of the Dixie Club,
> And happy we will be
> In our little shack by the railroad track,
> In number thirty-three.
>
> When our day's work is over,
> And there's nothing else to do,
> In that little shack down by the track
> Is the place for me and you.
>
> And we'll get Lew to make a stew,
> The stew we love so dear.
> And the Dixie Club will furnish the grub
> And a case of lager beer.

If we don't get home till morning,
We'll never care a damn
If the booze is in the bottle,
And the stew is in the pan.

But if the bottle is empty,
We must be on our way.
And the Jolly Five goes up the hill,
Just at the break of day.

Though our legs are kind of wobbly,
Our voices still are strong.
"We won't get home till morning"
Is the burden of our song.

And if a cop should spy us,
He pretends he doesn't see.
For he knows we are the Dixie boys
From number thirty-three.

Then here's good luck to the Dixie Club,
No matter where we roam.
And here's good luck to the Jolly Five
When we are far from home.

But if you're sad and lonely,
And this old world don't agree,
There's a welcome hand from that jolly band
In number thirty-three.

For hours they'd play and sing far into the night. When the last lantern was put out, the folks of Little Cove would walk slowly to their homes. There was a stillness in their hearts. They'd sleep hard and wake up strong for the next day of toil and sweat. It was a summer unlike any other. It was the season when music came to Little Cove. Then, like a whisper, the singers and their cart were gone.

5

HEADING NORTH

LITTLE COVE HAD no roads. There were only Indian trails and cart paths networking south to homesteaders. There was a turnpike ten or so miles south that lay east to west. Little Cove was out of the way to just about everything. There was the occasional Broadside that someone carried into town with news a month old. But only three or four could read a little. The townsfolk's interest in news from far away was limited. So an event known as the Civil War occurred without Little Cove hearing much about it.

They did hear about Abraham Lincoln. They'd heard about Africans who were slaves in the South. They heard about some fighting far to the south. But fishing and survival were their daily concerns. What was happening to others in distant parts didn't much concern the residents of Little Cove.

There was always a little excitement when someone new wandered into or through the small village. So a good many raised their heads when three African men and two African women arrived on a hot August day.

"Howdy, strangers. Where ya all heading?"

"North."

"Well, ya got a lake in front of yer. Hope ya don't plan on walking through it."

"That sure 'nough is a big, big lake. There don't seem to be no end to it. Where is the land out there? I can't see it. We been walkin' for quite a spell. Mind if we cool off?"

The five Africans walked to the shore. The women walked into the water, dresses and all. The men stripped off their shirts and joined them. They bobbed up and down in the cool waters of the great lake. There were sighs of relief.

As they came out of the water, everyone who had gathered around took particular notice of the bare backs of the three male Africans. Raised white scars zigzagged across their otherwise black skin.

"What the hell?" someone blurted out.

"Oh, we sorry."

"What the hell'd ya do to get those?"

The Africans stayed silent. Each wondered what kind of white men they were talking to. If they told the truth, if they said too much, would these whites put them in chains and sell them back south? Eventually one spoke.

"Masser put the whip to me 'cause I ain't pick 'nough cotton one day."

"You were whipped?"

"Yes sir, I was. We all was."

The men stared at one another with mouths agape. The African women looked down. Standing silently, the men put on their shirts.

An African broke the awkward silence. "We be awful hungry. We ain't et for near four days since we kilt a squirrel and a rabbit in the woods. We askin' for your Christian charity, sir. Iffen ya believe in the Good Lawd, if ya feel some kindness in yer hearts, we be much 'preciative iffen ya could spare some of yer food for us."

Bertha spoke up. "You all follow me. We have some good vittles a-cookin', plenty of fish and taters. We'd be honored if you'd join us for dinner."

The five Africans hadn't seen much kindness since they

ran away some weeks earlier. Their owners certainly showed none. It had been years since the whites arrived on the African shore. The blacks were dragged into the bilges of large ships and chained. None of the Africans could understand why the whites were so cruel to them. Why were they being taken from their tribes, their families? How could these whites believe in the sweet Jesus Christ and do the things they did?

But here in this Little Cove, they found friends willing to take them in, feed them, and give them shelter for rest.

Many of the regulars did not find their way to the tavern that night. Instead, most wandered over to Bertha's cottage. There they listened to stories far into the night. Hardened fishermen, nearly always ready for a fistfight or a scuffle, could hardly believe what the five Africans told them.

"What the hell?" they called out to the universe.

"What the hell? Were those slave owners human? Maybe they were really devils, Satan's own children."

They imagined themselves as slaves. What would they do? How many beatings would they endure before they would run? Not a fisherman in Little Cove had ever seen anything like it before. Not a fisherman in Little Cove could hardly believe the stories they heard.

"Go north. Go north until frozen white water covers the ground. Don't stop. Don't talk. Hide during the day. Run at night. Go north. Go north. We love you. We will never forget you. Go north."

The five Africans slept on the floor of Bertha's cottage that night. They didn't awaken until midmorning the next day.

"What will you do now?" Bertha asked while cutting slabs of smoked bacon.

"Well, 'spect we be heading north. But we don't know how we goin' get there with dat big water in da way. We ain't never done much fishin', so we can't stay here and be any hep. We real good at pickin' cotton. Don't see any cotton fields round these parts. We pretty good hunters if we got the right arrows and spears. The Good Lawd will show us da way. Don't know how it gonna be, but sweet Jesus take care of his chillen. Ya all witness to dat."

"Are you all from the same family?"

"Oh no. We not even from the same tribe. Dey mix us all up. Dey sell us off, dis one to dis masser, dat one to dat masser. Our wifes and chillen go dis way and dat way. We never see 'em again."

"So these aren't your wives?"

"Oh no, Missy Bertha. We just found dem along the way. Dey already run away from their massers. So we join up. We go north together. We bein' good Christian men; we honor their virtue. Dey sleep over der. We men sleep together here. We would kill a man now who try to bed one of deez women. I think the Good Lawd sent 'em our way so we can take care of 'em. Dat we done."

"What will you do when you get north, far enough away?"

"Oh, Missy Bertha, ya got lots o' questions. I don't think we rightly know what we gonna do. All we know is we gots ta get as far north as we can so our massers can never find us. We just know a better life be waiting for us. Ya know, the Good Lawd say dat in de holy book. He take care of his chillen like he take care of the sparrows dat fly. We all believe dat, just like you, Missy Bertha."

"Well, sometimes I don't know. We've had some hard, lean times here. We've been hungry a lot. The winters are so cold they can freeze the nose off your face. We don't have a church, but that don't mean we're not God fearers...well, most of us. Well, some of us. I think you Africans might be blessed with the faith gift more than most of us here in Little Cove."

"Ah, Missy Bertha, you know the Good Lawd love ya."

The men of the village went fishing that day as they did every day. The women mended nets and tended small gardens. The Africans just rested by the shore, looking out over the great body of water that lay between them and the far-enough North.

News traveled fast in Little Cove, maybe because there was so little of it. The men understood the deep desire of the Africans to run as far north as their legs could carry them. They understood. While they fished all day, their thoughts were "What should we do to help these poor, miserable people?"

During this time, the boats in Little Cove were small, built for one man, or at the most two. They were built for fishermen not ferrymen. But a couple of the larger boats could get them across to the northern shore.

That night, down at the tavern, the talk was about who would take them. Each considered whether he would volunteer. The men seldom talked about their deepest fears. They were, after all, strong fishermen. These were men who strove to live bravely. So the subject of the sea monster was never discussed. But deep down in their innermost being, all the fishermen knew there was one.

Their reasoning was simple. If God could create the sharp-toothed fish that lived in Sharp Tooth Lake; if God could create the ten-foot-long sturgeon that looked like a creature from ages past; and if God could create the ling, catfish, and mudpuppy, three of the ugliest swimmers one would ever see, then God could create a sea monster.

There was evidence. More than once, in deep water, a fisherman would feel a bump. His boat would heave up like something really big had swum underneath it. A couple fishermen even claimed they saw the sea beast breaching out in deeper waters.

Little Cove had witnessed brigs, schooners, ships, and sloops go by. But they were vessels thought to be far too large for a monster to take down. Their small fishing boats were another matter. Each one knew in the privacy of his own mind that the great sea monster could swallow his boat, and him with it, in one big bite.

In fact, nobody had ever sailed to the north shore from Little Cove, or so they thought.

"Well, Harry, Enis, why don't you two take 'em across? You have newer boats. You're a couple of the best sailors when it comes to rough waters. Your boats are bigger than ours. You're the right men. You have the right boats for the journey. We'll gather some provisions. You both can be off tomorrow. The skies look good for a few days."

Harry and Enis felt like they had been backed into a corner. They really couldn't say no and save face. It made sense, after all. They had the sturdiest boats. They were the best sailors. So each threw down another slug of whiskey and answered, "Sure, why not?"

Goodbyes were brief the next morning. The Africans waved. "The Good Lawd bless ya all," they said as they left. Sails were raised, and off they went. The breeze was strong from the southwest, the ideal push for where they were headed.

The folks in Little Cove were on edge all day. They didn't sleep well that night. "What if they don't come back?" It was a long way across. The great lake had a reputation of blowing up fast and mean.

By the end of the second day, they should have been back. Toward the end of day three, the whole village was worried. Not until midday on the fourth day were the two boats spotted upon the horizon. In a few hours, they made landfall in Little Cove.

"How'd it go, Enis?"

Enis looked pale. He paused before he said, "I ain't never ever goin' to do that again. I ain't never going that far out into the great lake. I ain't never going to cross that lake again as long as I live."

"What happened, Enis?"

Enis begged for confirmation as he looked toward the other man. "You saw it, Harry. You saw it under my boat as we went around the long point. You saw it swimming like, like a huge snake slithering along."

Harry admitted, "I saw something. It looked like a huge

dark glob of something. I couldn't tell just what it was. But, if you stacked all the cabins and huts together in Little Cove, this, whatever it was, was bigger. It moved from here to there. Then it was gone."

"I thought you saw it, Harry. It's out there. I know it is."

6

IT'S IN THE WRIST AND THE BLADE

"I'LL WAGER FOUR bits that Jenkins can clean ten fish in five minutes."

"You're on, you ol' scallywag."

"We're going to have to keep the time from the mantle clock at Bertha's place."

True enough. There were only a few timepieces in all of Little Cove. They all agreed that the official time would be from the clock at Bertha's Tavern. So they set up yellers to keep everyone posted from there down to the site of the contest. The place of that contest was the fish-cleaning dock in the small bay. This rickety structure jutting out into the water was where the women cleaned fish at day's end.

Down they went, running and scrambling. Several dozen crowded onto the cleaning dock, all a-whooping and a-hollering. This was the most exciting thing to happen in Little Cove in a month of Sundays, maybe longer.

"Any more bets a-fore we start this contest?" Calvin bellowed out.

It was one of those perfect summer days when life flowed strong through a man's body. They were all a little silly and testy. This could just as easily have been a good brawl—a dozen guys fighting for no better reason than to blow off steam. But this seemed just as good: a contest. The money was waving. The booze was flowing fast.

"Tell Bertha to count down," they yelled, relaying the message down to the dock. "Five minutes to go. "

"Five minutes to go," a voice echoed back.

"Four minutes to go."

"Four minutes to go."

Jenkins just stood there, cool as a clam, with his whetstone. He had put an edge on his knife like he'd always done. His blade was sharp enough to slice a hair lengthwise or cut a man deep if he'd a mind to.

"Why Jenkins cuts so fast, ya can't foller it with your own eyes. There's a hum a-comin' from his blade, I swear."

Everyone knew he was the best fishmonger in all of Little Cove, but to clean ten fish in five minutes? Well, the boys weren't sure even Jenkins was that good.

The excitement built. The whiskey, rum, and beer were going down faster than jiggers and mugs could be filled. Willie down at the tavern couldn't keep up with the pace. Up to the tavern and then back down he ran, trying not to spill the precious drinks.

Booze was one commodity Little Cove never ran out of, sustenance for the body and soul. The tavern had a stone basement. An iron door with a padlock as big as a man's fist kept the contents secure. Bertha hid the only key between those two sweet breasts of hers, night and day. She had a good blade to back off anyone who tried to steal it.

Nobody had ever been down to the storeroom, except one big, brawny fella, appropriately named Big Mike McCoy, who lugged the full kegs up and the empties down. Bertha had a special way to pay him to keep him honest. In Little Cove that tavern might just as well have been set over a diamond mine. That was the value of it to each one there.

"Three."
"Three."
"Two."
"Two."
"One. Start."

Jenkins grabbed the first fish. He started to carve. True enough, when there was a brief pause in the shouting, you could hear his blade hum. Everyone believed he heard the sound.

"Come on, Jenkins. You can do it."

Jenkins's hands flashed this way and that, but his face was relaxed. Some said he even looked peaceful. "He could have been a-laying in a hammock at sunset, sipping a beer," Colin said afterward. "Anybody else tried to clean a fish that fast, it wouldn't just be fish blood on the cutting board."

Three minutes in, Jenkins was already picking up his seventh fish. Now the fishermen in Little Cove weren't known for their intellect, but they knew their numbers. Jenkins was ahead of schedule. He was going to beat the clock.

"Dammit to hell," cussed Bucky. "I put down two bits and said he couldn't do it. Dammit, it looks like he will."

There was a groundswell of excitement as everyone crowded onto the dock to watch Jenkins at work. The yelling got to pushing and then shoving. The shoving got to tripping and then punching. Before you knew it, it was like twenty cats were a-scrappin' on a backyard fence.

Jenkins got bumped. He almost dropped the fish and his knife into the bay.

"Thirty seconds."
"Thirty seconds."

Jenkins had already made the two main cuts on the last fish. He moved on to gutting. Then creak. Crunch. Crack. *Crap!* The whole dock toppled over, broke apart, and fell into the bay. Folks were thrown this way and that. Little Cove bay got a big drink of whiskey that summer's day! There they all were, neck high in water, when they heard the bell from up at the tavern. The five minutes were over.

The whole crowd sloshed their way to the shore and attempted to reassemble and make some sense out of the chaos. "Well, did he finish or not?" a few yelled out. Some shouted, "Sure he did," while others shouted as loudly, "He didn't finish the last fish!"

"Why you damned liar, you. You catfish slime. You ugly bean farmer."

And so it went. The words brought shame to the heavens. Fists started flailing again. Down onto the sand they went. As there was no real leader in Little Cove to stop it, the fight went on for quite some time. Fights end, eventually. When the fellas got too weak to swing their arms and too thirsty, someone would usually blurt out, "Hey, guys, I'm tired of fighting. Let's get some drinks." So, off to the tavern they'd go, arms over each other's shoulders, laughing and dancing all the way. That was the way on this particular day as well. Men who one would have thought were going to kill each other, were now laughing, drinking, and singing songs far into the night.

There never was a decision, some final agreement about the outcome of the contest. Like so many issues in life, the definitive answer never came. They were left to wonder. They were left to mostly disagree.

Some say the fates were kind to the fishermen of Little Cove. Had it gone this way or that, what would there have been to talk, or argue, about during their long hours of fishing?

7

FREDERICK KARL PETTER NELSON

FREDERICK KARL PETTER Nelson was born on the island of Gotland in Sweden. He was born inland on a farm. They said he had seawater in his veins. So he became a sailor in his early teens. His trade was carpentry. He could fix anything wooden on a ship. He was a hunk of a man, six feet eight inches tall. He sailed around the world seven times. Once he was shanghaied in San Francisco and then released from impressment in Dublin.

They say, at some point, he jumped ship and ran inland, never to sail the oceans again. You'll soon know why. As a ship's carpenter, he assumed a midshipman's status on most vessels. That is, he did not sleep among the ordinary sailors on their berthing deck or among the commissioned officers in their individual, fairly comfortable rooms aft. He did occupy a private area—not a room but quarters, so named, probably, because the space was approximately one quarter the size of a land sleeping room. Most quarters were barely larger than a coffin. Bunks were customarily narrow and short. It was unusual to find a bunk more than five and a half feet long. Most were shorter. Whenever Frederick Karl Petter Nelson slept, there would be a good amount of him "hanging over."

GARY LARSON

In his status, he did not do the work of an ordinary sailor. His daily job was to take care of the wood. There was constant repair, replacement, varnishing, and painting. He, no doubt, observed some of the tasks of the ordinary seaman: bracing or sweating lines, or coiling a ballantine, but he had little experience in that line of work.

Frederick Karl weathered many squalls, storms, and even hurricanes from the comfort of his cabin quarters. It was the ordinary sailors who scampered up the ratlines to the upper spars to furl and reef in the sail. A brave task it was. One stood upon a rope stretched tightly under the spar, holding on with one hand. With the other free hand, he gathered the sail. This was done a hundred feet high off the deck as the vessel pitched to and fro. The sailors hung on for dear life. But "a ship is like a mother," the captains often taught. "You must take care of Mother so Mother will take care of you. Out upon the waters, it is only Mother who protects you from a drowning death in the stormy seas. When she needs our help, we protect her so she can protect us."

There was never a question about whether a sailor would go topside. "All hands on deck" meant everything was dropped and stopped, and every hand, including officers, captain, and carpenter, was needed.

On one terrible night, worse than any he'd experienced before, Frederick Karl Petter Nelson scrambled toward a mast. He looked up high. He started climbing his way up to the main topgallant yard. He shuffled his way out to the far starboard end of the spar. Never had he used more strength than on that night, hanging on to anything he could.

The ship pitched, rolled, yawed, and crashed. All that motion was hard enough down on the deck. Why a man could barely stand there below. But fifteen fathoms high upon a spar, the motion was magnified many times over.

The sailors were yelling to each other over winds that were screaming, groaning, and wailing over the vessel. The pitch-black night was occasionally broken by lightning strikes that illuminated an ocean in turmoil. The seas had built up from comfortable ten-footers to breaking waves forty feet high. The only hope was to bring in all sails and run bare spars downwind.

Then, in a split second, Frederick's foot slipped off the line, his hand released, and he fell into that angry sea. The sailors didn't stop their work even to look down. Their job was to finish their task. It was a life-and-death situation for all. Every sailor knew that death could happen in an instant. It was just the way. Frederick was lost.

On a calm day, floats could have been thrown toward the sailor in the water. With some maneuvering, some effort, and the tossing of rescue lines, an overboard sailor might be rescued. In a storm, there was nothing that could be done. Mother was screaming her need. The sailor was lost.

Yet, later, many a sailor testified to this truth. When the storm had ended, when they had ridden it out, as they gathered around the scuttlebutt to share in the story, they all agreed:

"It was a wave that did it. I never seen anything like it in all my life."

"It was like a big hand rising up out of the water. Frederick, I swear, was in that hand. That wave just threw him out of the sea and back upon the deck of the ship."

"What a lucky man that Frederick is."

"It's a charm to have him aboard, a good omen."

"Nah, it was the Almighty's providence, I say. It could be nothing less than that."

8

BEFORE THE WHITE MAN

LONG BEFORE LITTLE Cove was given its English name, a deep creek located two miles to the west ran to the lake. This creek connected the great lake to a large plateau lake with the Indian name Cutohan, meaning "sharp tooth." It was so named for an unusual fish seemingly found nowhere else.

"The lake god is not angry now. We should go to Sharp Tooth Lake while the weather is good," announced Manukah, the most experienced of the great lake crossers. "We should have a few days to fish before the next storm."

Twelve Indians in six white birch canoes gathered just enough supplies for a week's journey and paddled out from the northern shore. The lake crossing took little effort. Finding their portage creek presented more of a challenge.

"Do you see the white trees with the black spots up on the cliff? That's where the creek opening is," announced Manukah. Most grunted approval, but Eteah wasn't quite sure. The men paddled on. Waves were building on the lake, a typical chop for any day, but it created more of a challenge for small canoes.

There was little threat of human enemies. Only a handful of white men had arrived in the area. No other Indian would pose a problem as the council had built a treaty with most tribes. The peace pipe had been shared. There were no enemies except for black bears or mishaps. Sharp Tooth was not an enemy, but it was certainly dangerous.

As his canoe reached shallow water, Eteah stepped out. "The water is clear and cold," he said. All jumped in to cool off, splashing water over their perspiring bodies.

"Build a fire. We'll sleep by the creek tonight," Manukah announced. Driftwood was gathered. Tree moss and ferns soon became softer beds than sleeping on stones. Chunks of dried venison were eaten. A few stories were told around the campfire. All were reminded of the two huge buck deer that Tetewma killed just a week before that fed all of the tribe for days. While the story of the kill was told, a slight smile came over Tetewma's face as he settled down to rest.

Just before sunrise, Eteah was already stirring, aware that the land journey would be long. Each year a hunting party crossed the lake and portaged twenty miles to Sharp Tooth Lake to catch one special fish. Two men raised their canoe to their shoulders. With supplies in leather pouches, the journey began—up the high escarpment, then down, down to their secret, special fishing grounds. "Sharp Tooth" was the English name. Cutohan could be translated as "Lake of the Knife Tooth Fish" and shortened to Sharp Tooth Lake. Or Cutohan could refer to the fish itself. Lore has it that within the waters of this lake, a unique species of fish thrived. The Indians knew the fish could tear the arm off a man, cutting the flesh with sharklike teeth and snapping bones like twigs.

The Indians sought this fish for three reasons. First, the meat was firm and did not decay quickly. Second, some internal organs of the fish were used by medicine men to heal wounds and cure diseases. Third, within the skull of this unique fish, nature had shaped a nearly perfect round ball of bone that the Indians used to play many games. It was not only snow snake and lacrosse but also dozens of other games. These contests developed the strength of each brave. The skull ball of this strange but powerful fish was a prized treasure.

Noweepo had a sense of where to look in the lake, and he knew how to catch these fish. He was never bitten, not once. His respect for the great fish was so profound that he would never give up his guard. He taught the others how to handle and then kill this powerful beast. Even so, several Indians bore scars from struggles with and bites from cutohan.

There was always concern about when to stop fishing. The men not only had to carry the canoes back to the great lake, but also the extra weight of the fish in the boats. This was where the wisdom of Manukah came in as he judged the catch and estimated the additional weight against the strength of the twelve braves.

"We'll stop fishing now. Gather your gear for the journey back."

The portage back was broken up with several stops for rest. But they pressed on in a race against time. They knew fish could spoil, so they had to get their catch back across the lake where the women of the tribe would be waiting to process and preserve the precious meat.

Many wondered, in silence, if Manukah was right in his judgment of the weather cycle. Was there enough time to paddle back before the next big storm? Manukah felt the air upon his face. He watched the shapes and speed of the clouds going by. Even the bird songs signaled him to what might lie ahead.

"Hurry, hurry," urged Manukah.

Noweepo and Eteah had already fallen on the stones, but neither was injured much, except for their pride. "Ho yeh, Ho yeh," the others laughed as the two went tumbling down the creek bank. "Didn't you learn how to walk when you were young boys?" Tetewma chided.

They arrived on the beach late, but the lake was still roiling from the day's wind. They would have to wait for the wind to die down. In the middle of the night, the silence awakened Manukah. The breeze had died. The lake was flat.

All appeared safe for their return journey. One by one, the Indians awakened. All were told to pack up.

A quarter moon and many stars offered sufficient light for the travelers. They pushed off from shore. For a few hours, all went well. But shortly after the point of no return, more there than here, the great lake blew again. The natives were skilled at paddling through rough water. They knew how to cut the waves, to ride them. But suddenly a rogue wave caught Tetewmah and Noweepo by surprise. Their canoe flipped. Their entire catch sank quickly. But the two were able to splash enough water out of the canoe and climb back inside. All the other paddlers came closer to the two to be sure they were safe.

Paddling a canoe half full of water was more difficult than paddling a canoe full of fish. So the last leg of the crossing took much longer than anticipated. They reached the beach in the morning, guided by a large fire on their home shore that the tribe kept burning all night.

No one embarrassed Tetewmah and Noweepo for losing their fish. They had done the work. They risked the same as the others. They were part of the total effort to bring back food. The fishing journey of the twelve Indians was a success. No one had been injured or killed. All returned to their families. There was no thought or word about the loss of fish, only deep satisfaction over the catch. Many fresh fish would be eaten during the days ahead, but most would be stored for the winter. No one had to be thanked or honored, but at the next campfire, there would be much dancing.

Along with the dancing, the best storytellers would tell of various adventures.

"Koona saw a big black bear and screamed, and the bear ran away like a kicked dog." The children laughed. The women murmured to each other. "There was a big snake that tried to bite Arato. Arato killed the snake and ate him." Children jumped up, stamping their feet hard into the ground, licking their lips, and rubbing their stomachs. Arato was in those years between a boy and a man.

Stories became dances, and dances became stories as they were told and danced around the night campfire.

Stories of the big fish with the sharp teeth were always favorites. In the earliest stories, Sharp Tooth was as long as a man's leg. It bit like a dog. As the months and years rolled by, Sharp Tooth was as tall as a man. It bit like a buffalo. Then Sharp Tooth was as tall as four teepees. It bit like a sea monster, perhaps the same sea monster that bit out the land forming Little Cove. The children's eyes grew large. Wives and other women huddled closer to each other. Some put more logs on the fire to scare away Sharp Tooth should the beast try to swim into their camp. Children had nightmares of Sharp Tooth coming to eat them.

9

A WINTER'S REST?

AH, SLEEPY, RESTFUL winter? Maybe not. In Little Cove, winter began in late fall when ice formed over the lake. That could be anytime from December to April, or not at all. Fishermen fish until they are forced by nature to stop. When ice formed, fishing ended. The most temperamental weather arrived before ice formed and just after it melted. Gales were not uncommon in those in-between seasons called "spring" and "fall."

Once it had been determined that the fishing season was over, the task of hauling boats out of the water began.

No boat, wood or metal, can remain in the water when water becomes ice. No matter how big or strong the vessel, ice is stronger.

When water expands upon freezing and becomes ice, it crushes the hulls. So every boat must be hauled out of the water onto land. The smallest of boats, rowboats and skiffs, might weigh only a few hundred pounds, light enough that a few men can drag them up on shore with ropes. Two-masted fishing boats might weigh two tons or more. The all-enclosed metal fishing boat could top four tons. The task of pulling an eight-thousand-pound boat from water to land was a challenge.

Pulleys, block and tackle, pry bars, jacks, rollers, teams of mules, muscle, time, and effort—all of these, and more, were the tools used. Pulling a few dozen boats in freezing temperatures, often in sleet, hail, and snow, was an all-village effort that often lasted weeks. It was a desperate race to land them all before the lake froze solid.

"Ease off on the pulley rope. Lever that starboard side up a mite so I can get the jack under. Give the mule a nudge, and have her pull about two feet. Now get those rollers under; four of 'em should do. Watch out, Bucky! She's moving."

"Ah, piss and vinegar," Bucky yelled out. "The keel just took off two of my fingers."

"Are ya bleedin' much?"

"Eh, not too bad. Grab me a rag. I'll wrap up what I got left. Let's get that jack under here again. Straighten her up."

So it went. Why stop work for the sake of a couple of fingers?

Once the boats were on dry dock, was it time to rest? Not yet. There were repairs to be made to most boats. The minor repairs could be done in good weather, but only when the boats were out of the water could the undersides, planking, and keels be tended to. Leaks between planks had to be filled with oakum and tar. Broken spars, locks, tackle, and blocks needed repairs. Miles of rope had to be inspected and, if necessary, replaced. Repairing the fishnets was the women's task over the winter.

If there were a hiatus, it would be during the time between blocking up and repairing the last vessel, and the time when the lake ice was thick enough to cut. Once the thickness reached about a foot, the whole village focused on the task of refilling the ice house. Using swing saws and pendulum saws, they would cut blocks, then transport with horses drawn skids to the icehouse. The outside walls were a foot thick with timbers and rocks. The inside walls were covered with tin in later years.

"Bring in that sawdust and straw. Lay down a layer over that bottom level of ice. Make sure it's all covered. Now start the second layer. Work your way up. Ya gotta put a layer of sawdust and straw between each layer of ice, or it will never last through the fishing season. If ya squeeze out all that air, the ice will last."

"There goes Dom." Right down he went. "Can ya see him? He fell through the ice. Do you see him, boys? Watch out; don't get too close to the hole, or you'll be going through too. I don't see him at all. Can you see him? Tie on an anchor and drop it down through the hole. If he's still moving, he can grab the rope. Then we'll pull him up."

A short time passed. Everybody knew. Dom was done.

The men were sawin' out blocks some distance from where Dom went through. They pulled out some chunks and up popped Dom. "Like a cork comin' up out of the water, there he was."

The men pulled him up and out and laid him on a skid. The horses were harnessed, ready to go. Pete stayed on the skid to keep Dom from falling off. Jake grabbed the whip. They were off to Bertha's Tavern. They carried Dom in. He was as stiff as a board.

They laid him down in front of the roaring fireplace. The women went to work. A dozen women rubbed his skin, moving his arms and legs.

"Come on, Dom, you ol' buzzard. You get back to us right now.

Goddamn it, you're too young to cash out your hand. Start breathing, you poop, or I'll kill ya."

Dom opened his eyes, coughed out a bucket of lake water, and said,

"Did I drink too much? Why are you all looking over me? Can ya get me a blanket? I'm mighty cold!"

Once the icehouse was full, was it finally time for some winter rest?

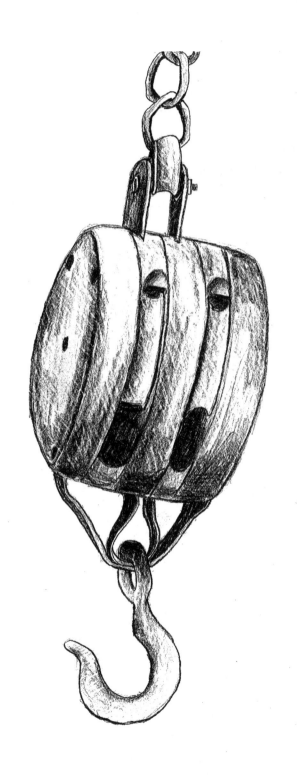

Someone shouted out, "The firewood piles are nearly gone. We've got months left of cold weather. Get some teams and sleds. Get back to that place by the gorge, and start sawin' up those hardwoods that we felled last spring. You wanna be warm? Then get your arses going. We need wood, and we need it now."

The Mrs. chimed in with her two cents, "How am I supposed to cook without firewood, you lazy bums?"

In just days, it would be spring again. Time to fish.

10

THE PHILOSOPHER

THERE HE STOOD. It seemed like he came out of nowhere. He was quite tall, quite thin, and quite noticeable. He wore a three-piece suit, shiny shoes, and a black top hat. His eyes were too large for his face. His nose was so long, he would have bumped it looking sideways. He had a long, pointed goatee. He held a cane. And he had one of those funny little monocles squished in front of one eye.

"Good day. Top of the morning to you, my good lads. Say, what place is this?"

Butch, Hank, Jerry, and Shane just happened to be walking by together. They stopped going to wherever it was they were going.

"Uh, this is Little Cove."

"Well, it appears to be that, indeed. Allow me the honor of introducing myself. I am Cornelius Radcliffe Waldorf III; that's the third, mind you. I am a philosopher. A philosopher, my good fellows. From the Greek word *phil*, meaning love, and *sophos*, meaning wisdom. I live for the love of wisdom. I explore the meaning of existence, the purposes of life. I immerse my being in thought and reason. My good men, I am, therefore I think."

"You don't fish or nothing?" Jerry blurted out.

"You don't work? Do you farm or hunt or do anything?" Hank inquired.

"My work, my life, is thought, my good men. But enough of this. Can you see I am hungry and thirsty? Are there God-fearers in this village who can offer me a meal?"

"Well, you can go on up the hill there to Bertha's Tavern. She's always got a kettle of stew on the fire and some beer for your thirst."

"No cognac or kippers?"

Shane whispered to Butch, "What kinda fella is this guy? Who is this Corney Rad...whatever fellow?"

"I say, chap, get it right. Cornelius Radcliffe Waldorf III."

A few of the men in Bertha's covered their mouths, so as not to burst out laughing at the sight of this strange-looking character. Others turned away in an unusual attempt to look uninterested.

"I understand you serve a proper meal for the sojourner, Miss Bertha?"

"Sure do."

"Well, I'll have a plate of whatever is your very best of meals," he said. "Now, if you'll all gather around, chaps, we'll begin today's lesson. You see, gentlemen, upon reflection, in a sense life makes no sense. The man who smiles the most is the saddest of all men. A person can be as wealthy as a shah and still not sleep at night. The beauty of nature is dashed as coyotes eat a deer alive. The most civilized men kill other men. We go to war for peace. We mind our own business and still get into trouble. What we think in one moment to be hardship later becomes a blessing. We give it our best effort and still fail. We desperately desire to be accepted, but we do not accept others.

"'Why is it that the evil I would not do, that I do, and the good that I would do, I don't do?' lamented the good Apostle Paul. When we think all is lost, we are found. As we face the end, it becomes a new beginning. A mountain becomes a molehill, and then a molehill becomes a mountain. The sea's waves break down the mountain, and the mountains rise up to create more seas. We eat and fill our stomachs only to be hungry again. We sleep and dream, unable to make any sense of it. Are you catching the drift, gentlemen? Life makes no sense. It defies reason."

"I am a man who spends his life in reason. For what?" Koehleth cried out, "Vanity, vanity, all is vanity. Why do the good suffer and the evil prosper? Evil men live four score and ten, while the good man is cut down in his prime. What is the sense to any of it?"

"Ah, I perceive the glazed look of men trying to understand. Stay with me, boys. There is no sense to sense. There must be a different way, a higher way. But what is it? Shall we simply satisfy our passions like brutes? Shall we care not to understand our universe? Shall we drown our thoughts with wine and the lust of women to dull our senses? Nay. They are fruitless choices. So what then shall we do? Shall we deny the paradoxes and enigmas of life? Shall we press on as if they don't exist? Like the ostrich in Australia, shall we bury our heads in the sand, pretending that reality is not present?

"What then are other options? Have you thought, men? Shall we be daft, electing stupidity? What say, ye? Consider deeply, men.

"Ah, I see the pork and potatoes have arrived for my consumption. I will assume that you chaps will cover my tab. A man so blessed in thought as I need not be bothered with monetary matters. So, hie thee on. Let me dine in peace. Oh yes, I shall need a room in this place, as I have nowhere to rest my head. Shall we see you in the next day and continue our talk?"

The men backed away, dazed. These were words they'd never heard, thoughts they'd never thought. It was like there was an explosion of TNT in Bertha's Tavern that night. Nothing had so upset their routines. They were amazed, speechless.

They did drift back to their tables. They looked on from a

distance as Cornelius daintily devoured his meal. The chaps finished their drinks and slipped out quietly to their homes, whispering as they left.

"What man is this to come our way?"

"These fancy words he has, I lose myself in them."

"He talks so queer. I thinks it's English, but I can't be quite sure."

"I catch some of his meaning, but then I'm lost."

"Imagine, not working, only thinking!"

"Do you think we're safe with the likes of him around?"

"I saw no gun, nor knife. I doubt he'd know what to do with either."

"My head's a-spinnin'. I'm not sure I'll sleep tonight."

"What kind of name is Cornelius Radcliffe Waldorf, anyway? Where do you think he's from?"

"Perhaps our Good God dropped him down from the stars as a misfit from heaven."

"How can sense not make sense? Well, there's no sense to it. If sense isn't sense, what is it?"

Many different ideas were swirling around that night, but to a man, they were all curious to hear more. There was something this Cornelius came to give. They all were of a mind to receive it.

The next day was like every other day: fishing all day and then gathering at Bertha's Tavern for a few beers and some man talk. Some were eager to play cards, but more wanted to hear that Cornelius chap ramble on with his ideas. It didn't take much encouragement before all of the men had moved their chairs to Cornelius's table as he finished his evening meal. Dabbing his mouth with a napkin rag while sticking his pinky finger out in a most peculiar way, he gazed at those assembled.

"Good day fishing, lads? There's a distinct odor that gives you away. So nice to see you all again. Am I presumptive to believe you gentlemen are gathered for an evening discourse?

Well, of course, you are here for that. Like chicks gathered to the mother hen, your empty craniums are yearning to be filled with the wisdom that only I can impart. So, listen on, my good men. Be attentive. Better yourselves.

"When we are born, our abrupt awakening, as it were, is the disconnection from our mothers. Disconnections are usually accompanied by wails and crying. Snip goes the mother's cord that was connected to the child. We are separated from all that was our entire source of life. That tie is severed. Never again shall we know that sense of oneness, although we will search to regain it from the moment of our first breath.

"From birth begins the brief illusion that we are the world and the world is us. Everything we see, hear, smell, taste, or touch is just an extension of 'me,' or so we think. But gradually or suddenly, we come to know that there is some disconnecting going on. This is why we cry, flailing about so uncontrollably, when our mothers leave. 'There goes me,' we think. 'We want me back.' After all, I am fed by me, cuddled by me. I enjoy me. But now me is not giving me what I want by leaving. Perhaps she's in the privy?

"We want childhood friends to be like us. When they're not, we have fights and throw dirt. We are especially upset when they take our toys and won't give them back. They are disconnecting us from our sources of pleasure. We don't like it. It does seem, as we wander through life, that those we like—those who become our friends—are very like us. There may be opposites, but that just reflects the paradoxes of our characters. It's simple: we like some people; we don't like others. I would suggest that those we like are like us. We want to surround ourselves with dozens of other 'me's.' We want me to be with me everywhere me goes. We don't really like those other people.

"Love and marriage are queer things as well. The intimate act of, shall we call it, physical union is simply our attempt to make one thing out of two things, to reconnect with that part that has been disconnected from us. For a few moments of passionate bliss, we believe, we are one again, but that soon fades. Indeed, for most people who have stood at the marriage altar and taken their vows, in later years they can't remember why they did it. The feeble attempt at reconnection seldom if ever lasts. Most are depressed that they ever tried it with one or a dozen other partners.

"But, as we're rolling along, entertaining this idea and that, we conceive that we would like to create children. Me friends and me lovers don't seem to meet the need, so we create me children. 'The acorn doesn't fall far from the tree,' as the saying goes. But children invariably disconnect from us as well. They are with us and part of us for a season, but then they move on. They separate from us, physically, emotionally, in every way.

"Let's use the metaphor of a tree. We all begin with a common trunk and roots. Let's call it the tree of life that we are all a part of. But as we grow, we send out our own branches and leaves. These are formed by our life experiences, thoughts, and personal histories, each one unique from all others. In a way, we're all alike. We are all leaves on various branches. But the me leaf is not the you leaf. Many come to understand that. Some never will. With each day of living, we become more separated from every other thing because our unique lives are so unlike any other life. We are disconnecting. We are disconnected. We try to come together, but our attempts are futile.

"What friends we make in life begin to die off, one by one. The list of disconnections becomes larger. Then comes our time to die, the final disconnection. It's ironic how our first big disconnection is at birth, and our last big disconnection is at death."

Walt cried out, "Bertha, bring over another round of beers. Bring a bottle of whiskey too."

"Does this all make sense, gentlemen?"

Everyone nodded yes. Then they all shook their heads no.

"None of us has been to school, Corney. Your words are big ones. Your ideas are bigger still. What I think we're trying to say here is we gets parts of your words, here and there, but most of it just don't make any sense. Like you said the other night, there ain't no sense to sense."

"You are children in the art. Perhaps, in time, these thoughts of truth will find some growth in your very infertile minds. No offense, men."

"None taken."

"What's an infertile mind?" they whispered to each other.

After fishing the next day, a few of the men were at the scuttlebutt chattering.

"How'd you do with the catch?"

"Oh, not so bad."

"A little bumpy out there today."

"Well, good enough wind to sail back in."

"Say, where's that philosophy feller?"

"Nary a soul has seen him all day."

"Guess he must have wandered off early. God knows what town will get him next. Heard he never paid his bill down at Bertha's. 'Course I don't think he ever intended to."

"Got nets to fix. Tore some big holes."

"My boat's up on the rollers. Been leakin' heavy. Need some hot tar in the cracks."

"Guess I'll take a pass on the beer tonight."

"Yeah, me too."

"Yeah, me too."

11

RUBY AND CHARLIE

"**ARE YOU UP** there, Ruby? Are you awake? Can I see you?"

"Who's calling me?"

"It's Charlie Miller. Can I see you?"

"Give me a minute. I'll be down to unlock the door...You just passing by, Charlie, or do you want to come in?"

"Well, if it's no bother to you, I come for a visit."

"A visit?"

"You know, I like to talk too...You got such a pretty place here, Ruby. Soft things. Pictures on the wall. It always smells so good here."

"Is that what you came by to tell me, Charlie, that my house suits your eyes and nose?"

"I'm just trying to be civil."

"I'm surprised you know that word. Do you know what it means?"

"I ain't fighting with you, am I?"

"That's as good a definition as any, I suppose...So what you been up to, Charlie?"

"Oh, just fishing and stuff. You know, what a fella does day after day. Sometimes I just get tired of it all. There's no excitement. Everything is always the same. I suppose that's why I come by to see you, Ruby. You put a change in my living, a good change. I don't like fighting all the time, in spite of what they say. So that's what I'm here for, Ruby."

"You do seem to fight a lot."

"Well, it's the guys. They make fun of me. They're always teasing. They get me so mad I feel like I got fire in my belly."

"What do they tease you about?"

"Well, you know."

"If you don't tell me, I can only imagine."

"Well, then imagine, and that's it."

"Oh, Charlie, let it go, will you? I've seen lots of men over the years. There's only two kinds: big and big enough. I'd say you're big enough to put a smile on a girl's face."

"Ah, they never stop. If it's not this, it's that. They know I'll fight if they make me mad enough."

"Charlie Miller, you do have the reputation of being the village fighter, hands down. How many times has the barber sewn you up? You've got scars on just about every part of your body. There's hardly a fisherman whose knife hasn't given you a slice somewhere. Are you ever going to stop?"

"Not if they keep teasing. Fact is, I'm a sight, ain't I? I know I'm not easy to look at with clothes off. My face is bad enough, but there's hardly a spot on my body that isn't scarred. That's why I don't want to come here, Ruby, 'cause I'm ashamed. I want you, but I know it ain't easy giving comfort to a man like me."

"Charlie, you know I never had much. Papa left, and Mama plied the same trade as me. It's all we kind can do. We weren't born with money. Ain't no frilly lace in our family tree...just broken branches. I never went to school. I can't do much more than write my name. When I came here years ago, this was the first place that didn't run me out of town. I needed Little Cove. I think the guys needed me. I lead a grateful life, Charlie. It may not seem so. I don't get much excitement in my day either, but I got a roof over my head and food on the table.

"Anybody comes in and starts laying it on me, saying mean

things like 'Ruby, the only good position you know is on your back,' or 'Ruby, you're not as good as a two-bit whore,' well, that's the last time ol' Ruby will comfort them. There's only been two these many years. You'll never see Ruben or Stig in my place again. I never did like being called 'a common lady.' But the rest of the fellas have all been gentlemen to me. They all know how to treat a lady. They know I won't ever tell their wives. They're appreciative, and I charge a fair price.

"See, Charlie, we have to learn to look at the inside of a person. Seeing just the outside allows a person to make a quick judgment. That judgment is often wrong. It takes some time to find the inside, to understand what's going on. Some folks think my whole life revolves around the outside of a man— how tall and handsome he might be; if he's dark, hairy, and smells like...oh, I don't know what that smell is, but it draws a woman and opens her up. Well, I'm not just interested in that. I want to come to know the inside of a man, whether he's got any courtesy in him or not, whether he thinks about anybody other than himself. So, I can look beyond the outside, Charlie. I don't see your banged-up old body. I see the good man in you."

"Ruby, I don't know what to say."

"You never have been much for words."

"Ruby, I don't know which of us had it worse. My daddy was drunk every day. He was mean. He'd beat Mama, Billy, and me until we couldn't walk. He'd eat, and we'd all go hungry. He didn't give a shit about anyone or anything. I almost killed him once. I stood over him passed out on the floor. I had a butcher knife in my hand. I pleaded with Mama and Billy, 'Let's just kill the bastard and leave.' But they wouldn't. I don't know why, but they couldn't. Then I left. I was fourteen years old. I never looked back. I ran for weeks till I was goddamned sure that shithead would never find me. That's how I ended up here in Little Cove. When Whitey asked, 'What you do for work, fella?' I looked around, saw the boats and nets, and said, 'I'm a fisherman.' Whitey said, 'We need men like you here.' That's how I got here. It's been going on twenty-five winters since then."

"Now, Charlie, I don't know what to say."

"Ah, Ruby, the fights I get into now ain't nothing compared to the beatings from my old man. I like the fellas I fight with here, so the pain from them ain't so bad. But I hated my father. That hate made each punch he gave me hurt all the more. How does God make a man so mean, Ruby?"

"How about a whiskey? I think we both could use one."

"Never would a whiskey taste so good as now. All these years we've been seeing each other. Only now we get to know each other a little. How can that be?"

"The inside takes time, Charlie. You can't rush it. It's got its own time, not like the outside time. You had to trust me. I had to trust you. That doesn't happen overnight."

"Could I have another shot, Ruby? It just tastes like a different kind of drink. Most times I drink to cover the pain, to make me forget. This whiskey makes me feel like I'm at a church wedding. Too bad we don't have a church, right, Ruby? I don't know if you ever been to one, Ruby, but a church wedding is quite a thing. Folks is smiling so much they're crying. After the parson joins hands, there's a feast like you never been at before. The food tastes so good. The whiskey tastes so good. It's happy whiskey. It's lift-a-glass-high whiskey. It's full-of-hope whiskey. That's how this whiskey tastes now. Ruby, I'd surely like one more if you'd have one with me."

"I certainly would, Charlie. Here's to you. Skoal."

"Skoal to you."

"I think we've been sitting here a long time."

"Yes, we have."

"I'm just sitting here, smiling, happy. I can't remember when I've felt like this before. Most times I want to end. Time now, I don't want to end."

"We got all night, Charlie."

After a long silence, they got up from their chairs at the same time and walked upstairs to Ruby's bedroom. On either side of the bed with their backs to each other, they undressed. Then they turned and faced each other. They slid into bed, lying naked next to each other, and pulled the covers up on the cold night. Time passed.

"What's your last name, Ruby?"

"It's just Ruby. That's all."

"You don't have a last name?"

"I had a last name, but I hardly remember it anymore."

"So, all the name you have is Ruby?"

"That's it."

"Well, is Ruby your real name?"

"No."

"You ain't Ruby?"

"Yeah, I'm Ruby now, but I wasn't always Ruby."

"You mean you gave yourself the name Ruby?"

"That's right. When I came to Little Cove years ago, I introduced myself as Ruby. Nobody ever asked for more. Ruby is a pretty name, don't you think? I suppose I could have been Pearl or Jade, but I like Ruby. I'm a jewel, you know. I've never even seen a real ruby, but there's times I feel as if I am one. I never did like the name I was given."

"Well, that's all I've ever known you by. It'd be hard to think of you now as Helen or Rachel. You ain't going to believe this, Ruby. But I'm not Charlie Miller. I hated my name. Hugo...Hugo Mosakowski. What kind of a dumb name is that? When I came to Little Cove, they asked who I was. I said, 'Charlie, Charlie Miller.' I don't know where that name came from, but it seemed to just slide out from somewhere inside of me. Charlie Miller. It's one of the few things I've liked about myself. Don't you think it's a nice name, Ruby?"

"It's a fine name, Charlie. It seems to suit you."

"Good night, Ruby."

"Good night, Charlie."

Morning came. They both awakened, smiling. They stretched, got out of bed, and started to get dressed.

"Can I get you some breakfast before you leave, Charlie?"

"That would be fine."

"How's some hardtack, coffee, and a couple raw eggs?"

"Oh, that sounds good."

"You know you've already missed the boats leaving for the day. They'll be fishing today without you."

"Something else to tease me about."

"You could catch up if you get going."

"I just don't feel like I want to leave, Ruby. I wish we were... I wish we...you and me...I wish we was together."

"We are together, Charlie."

"Oh, not like that, Ruby. I wish we was together for all nights. I wish we was together for every night and every day. I wish you and me were...well, you know."

"What are you trying to say, Charlie?"

"I know it won't ever happen. No one wants to be with a man the likes of me all the days. I just wish we were man and wife, Ruby. I wish we were...married."

"Well, four thirty in the morning and I'm getting a marriage proposal?"

"I'm not saying I'm asking, Ruby. I mean...well...maybe I...I just wish we were like we was all last night, close beside each other, keeping each other warm."

"I'll have to think about this, Charlie, but you know it wouldn't work."

"It wouldn't work?"

"As much as I care about you, Charlie, I've got the other men to think about as well. They like to come by too. How would that be for you?"

"Well, if we was married, Ruby, I wouldn't stand for any other man coming around."

"Well, lots of men been coming around for a long time, Charlie. It'd be hard to change all that."

"Well, I suppose. But you just make all of me feel right, Ruby. You set me back on the firm ground. I know who I am again when I'm with you."

"I like you too, Charlie, scars and all. I know I'll be seeing you again. But be sure to call out first. Make sure I'm not busy with some of my other responsibilities. Those fish are calling for you, Charlie. You best get going. You come back to see me again when you need to see me again."

"Ruby, can I tell you that I—"

"No, Charlie, don't use those words. They're very, very special words. Not everybody can say them. Not everybody can hear them. So, let's just say goodbye for now. Let's remember the time we had, our time."

"Well, OK then, Ruby. I'll see you again. You take care of yourself."

"You as well, Charlie. Time to go catch those fish."

Charlie went out the front door and walked down the lane. It was still dark. Immediately he was jumped by two men who beat him unconscious. Seems as though they both wanted some of Ruby's time that night as well.

12

FRENCHIES

THERE ONCE WAS a time when men in black robes and men in brown robes roamed the land and paddled the waters. Their intention was to bring religion to what they called the "heathens." They brought a new language and their culture, and they brought disease. They were French, mostly.

Over time a new breed of Frenchmen arrived, known generally as the "mountain men." They received that name because they became rugged, independent, strong, and fearless. They were employed by European companies that had an endless market for just about any kind of fur.

Overtrapping reduced populations, so the mountain men traveled west, walking upon worn Indian paths, if they were lucky, or through continuous woods. They walked, pushing handcarts or pulling mules heavily laden with supplies and furs. Others paddled canoes along the shorelines of the greater lakes, and along connecting rivers and streams. Fur-trapping mountain men passed through Little Cove every now and then. Most were only there for a brief stopover to hire a whore or resupply for the next leg of their journey.

"We don't have many women in Little Cove, Frenchie."

"Well, I'll pay for what you have."

"That'll be twenty cents, a dime more for the room upstairs."

Sophia smiled at the stranger as they ascended the stairs. They walked into a room with only candlelight.

Little Cove was hard to find, even for the wilderness mountain men. They were only given these instructions: "follow the shoreline till it raises up to a bluff that runs a three-day walk." On a clear day, one could see all the way to the other shore from that bluff, although one's eyes had to be as good as a hawk's. Even so, a good spotter could identify a grove of trees, a bay, or a darker hue that indicated land not water. It was an easy walk. As they trod along, the waters seemed to change colors before them—green, blue, and brown.

Although the residents of Little Cove considered themselves decent, God-fearing people, they had no church. "Don't need no religion here," Zack announced. "Don't need no preaching, no Bible reading here. If a priest shows up, we'll drive him out."

So there was no baptizing, no marrying. Burying occurred without pomp or ceremony. The deceased were lowered down. Mother Earth was piled on to make sure the stink stayed down. Those who were gathered walked away in silence. Maybe a few sentences were spoken.

"That bastard never could fish."

"He was more lazy than working."

"Good riddance to him."

Those would be considered kind accolades to what was often a man's only eulogy.

A few of the Frenchies stayed on. They tried to fish, but they were poor at it. Most wanted the furs and the money that came with them. It wasn't just beaver and mink the trappers sought. They'd trap and tan a dozen other critters.

Some trapped what they could in the woods near Little Cove. But there were reminders of times when things went wrong. One Frenchie clopped around Little Cove for years. He wasn't fit to push further west since he fell prey to his own hidden trap. Bear traps were sharp and exceedingly powerful.

They were set and hidden under leaves, so it was easy to forget just where they were. Jean Depew Trouleanu, who was only known as Frenchie, experienced a trap firsthand, or should it be said, first foot? On a late November day, he dragged himself back to Little Cove with his foot snapped clean off by a bear trap.

"Get that fire torch. Burn that leg shut before he bleeds clean out."

"Well, he passed out. Lucky he did."

He survived and hobbled with a crutch until his last breath. He was fed by the townsfolk but mostly ignored, even shunned.

"What stupid pup would walk into his own trap?" That was as kind as the fishermen could be. The French were not highly regarded at all.

Thousand-pound bears were common. One of the Frenchies was killed, clawed up, and chewed almost beyond recognition.

"Merde, du sang," Timothee Boucher blurted out when he came upon Liam in the woods. "Shit and blood all over." They didn't even bother to bury the pieces. Parts of Liam were spread here and there.

Jacques Farley passed through Little Cove, a muscular giant of a mountain man. He was already a legend, well known for bringing back the highest-quality pelts. He was eager to go west again where the trappin' was still good.

"Mon Dieu," Matty blurted out when Jacques came through the tavern door, no doubt overcome by his massive size. Jacques didn't answer but drank down a couple rums and walked back out.

"Who's that jackass think he is talking to me?" Jacques shouted to an unsuspecting passerby. To Jacques Farley, all the people in Little Cove were nothing more than stupid fishermen. He wasn't the first Frenchie to feel that way.

What the Frenchies didn't realize was that the disdain

went both ways. The fishermen thought the Frenchies were arrogant. Their contempt for them ran deep. The locals would often give inaccurate directions and information to the Frenchies. They'd water down their whiskey. They'd over-charge for supplies.

"I just don't like 'em," Billy confided to Red.

"Eh, they can drink piss as far as I'm concerned."

"I never met a Frenchie I liked."

"They're a dishonest lot, they are."

"Stupid too."

13

FEAR THAT MAKES
A MAN QUIVER

NO MORTAL LIVES without fear. If a man says he's not afraid, he's a damned liar or a fool. He has no self-concept or understanding of why he does what he does.

A cow experiences fear but doesn't know what it is. A bird feels fear, but the idea of what fear is, is unknown. By contrast, a person feels fear and knows that what he feels is fear. It is the idea that makes man different from all of the other beasts.

We fear pain. We fear death. We fear being with people. We fear being alone. We fear failure. We fear the dark. We fear the known. We fear the unknown. The list of fears is a long one.

That being said, fishermen have one fear, or at least the fishermen of Little Cove had but one fear. A person from the outside might think there would be more.

A person might think, "Perhaps the fisherman would fear getting a fish hook impaled deeply into his body. Perhaps they would fear hunger. Perhaps they would fear being lost on the lake. Perhaps they would fear a fistfight or a knife fight with another whose sole intent was to hurt them."

The fishermen of Little Cove feared none of this. They had lived too hard a life to fear these small threats.

Shakespeare wrote in *Macbeth*, "I am the Thane of Cawdor. If good, why do I yield to that suggestion whose horrid image doth unfix my hair and make my seated heart knock at my ribs, against the use of nature? Present fears are less than horrible imaginings."

It is the thought of fear, of horrible imaginings, that puts us on edge and unsettles us.

So, a yarn, an event really, occurred hundreds of times in Little Cove and certainly not by accident. For it was the horrible imaginings of the fishermen that created yet more horrible imaginings in the minds and hearts of visitors to Little Cove.

It was the darkest of nights, moonless and still. Two companions were riding horses through deep woods, endeavoring to arrive someplace friendly to spend the night. The horses trotted along single file down a narrow path, feeling the bushes and tree leaves as their only way of knowing where the path was and which way to go. Night sounds surrounded them: owls, crickets, the rustling of leaves.

"Holy Mother of God, what is that?"

"What, Hal? What do you see in Christ's name?" shouted the rider behind the lead horse.

"Oh my God, my God. Do you see it?"

"See what? I can't see a thing in this cursed darkness."

The horses stopped. The two men craned their heads from side to side and strained to bring into focus anything that might make sense. The horses snorted and stomped their front hooves. They were spooked too. They waited. They waited for something to happen. They reached for their pistols but kept them holstered.

"It doesn't seem to be moving."

"What the hell do you see?"

"I don't know. I don't know. Be quiet. Shhh."

The horses began to settle down and just stand. The riders sat, waiting. Nothing happened, but there was clearly something there the likes of which neither had ever seen.

The lead rider dismounted. He reached for the kerosene lantern tied to the back of his horse along with other gear. He fiddled with a match and lit the lantern. He turned to hold it up.

"Jesus save us. Have you ever seen anything like it?"

Both men attempted to compose themselves. They breathed heavily. But this thing that they were gazing upon was motionless. It made no sound. They walked slowly forward to a large dead tree, barren of leaves but covered in the devil's own handiwork. Before them, nailed to every branch of this tree, were several hundred heads of fish skulls. Their mouths were open, their sharp teeth showing. The flesh had long ago been eaten off by birds and insects. The men gazed upon these many white skulls of large fish. It seemed as if they were standing in front of the gateway to hell.

"What kind of place is this?" one said to the other. "Who would do this thing and why?"

After a time, they remounted their horses but kept the lantern lit. They continued down the narrow path. Little did they know that it was the only path into Little Cove, twisting and turning through the east woods until it opened into the village. They could see the lights from cabins in the distance, but they were unsure what they might find.

No one entered Little Cove without notice. Once seen, the word passed quickly to all the fishermen of the village. Out from their cabins and the tavern they filed to greet the next folks passing through.

"Welcome, strangers. Are ya passin' through or stayin' a spell?"

"We're not rightly sure, but we could sure use a stiff drink, some food, and a place to lay our heads for the night."

So the conversation evolved as it had hundreds of times before. Finally, the subject was broached.

"Following that path into town tonight, we came upon a sight that scared the bejeebers out of us both. You know what I'm talking about? Just a mile or so east of your town?"

"You wouldn't be talking about the fish heads, would you?"

"If that's what you call that monstrous totem. What the hell is it for?"

"Well, it's one of them different things, to be sure, a little hard to explain. We never know for sure who will be riding into our little village. They might be people of good upbringing, or they might be scoundrels. If they be scoundrels, often they don't come no farther than those fish skulls. They turn around and hightail it off in another direction once they've laid eyes on our little welcoming tree. But God fearers? They know part of the faith life is facing monsters and livin' with 'em. So they generally find the courage to keep on comin'. We take it that you are friends, not foes. It's as simple as that."

The visitors sat in silence for a while to take in the idea. The explanation seemed somehow inadequate.

"Can you go on, brother? We're thinking there must be more to this story."

So Daniel, one of the better spokesmen, continued over a few beers.

"Well, friends, if you mosey down to the water's edge in tomorrow's daylight, you'll find another tree just at the channel out to the lake. There you'll see another dead oak tree, as big as the other one, filled with just as many skulls of dead fish. It is sort of a totem, a protector. It stands guard day and night to scare off any denizen in the lake who might be hungry for human flesh."

"Whatever do you mean? A sea creature that feeds on humans?"

"Well, sir, we think it's out there."

There was a long silence among the men. They lit their pipes, fiddled with their beer mugs, and shuffled their chairs, but nobody spoke.

"I know you fellers might think you've just rode into a village of loonies, but we aren't crazy. We're just honest fishermen. Been fishin' this lake and others for years. We're telling you the truth. We've seen things, things that make a man know what fear really is."

By this time, ain't nobody going to walk through the dark night from the tavern back to their cabins. The "thing" that was always present but seldom talked about had captured the imagination of every person there.

So Daniel kept talkin' 'cause there was only one thing to do with fear once it was there inside the circle. It had to be faced and faced down.

"This cove has been here for hundreds of years. Long before we white men arrived, the Indians fished around here. They didn't call this place Little Cove. To them it was *Katch Uneh*, which translates pretty closely to 'big bite.' Legend has it that there has been a great sea monster swimming around this lake since the beginning of the Good Lord's creation. This creature, while chasing some prey, opened its huge mouth, bit into the land, and took a giant chunk out of the shoreline. That's how Little Cove, our home, was created."

"Oh, now those things are just stories, just myths and legends. We know there's no beasts out there like that."

Daniel looked straight ahead, and the others look down.

"With all due respect, this is a fable. The Indians filled their campfires with hundreds of such stories. All, not true. None of them. Not true."

Daniel continued, "May I tell you about something that happened just a few years ago?"

"Proceed."

"Ships pass by this harbor all the time taking immigrants west to settle and farm. There's schooners, barques, cutters, and steamships. Not all of them make it to their destinations. There's a good many things can take a ship down out there. About three miles west from here we found a ship breaking up on the shore. Alex and an old Indian, name of Long Hands, came riding back to Little Cove yelling that we had to come quick. Pretty much the whole village headed out. I'll tell you what we saw, fellas.

"We'd seen 'em washed up before, but this one was a little different. There were boxes and crates scattered all over the beach. The rigging on the masts was danglin', sail canvas was all over, but there was no sign of dead people. We walked up and down the shoreline. A couple fellas went through the vessel. There was not one dead human body—and by the way, no pigs or chickens either. Well, it was quite a mystery. We could tell the ship was only there a day or so. Where were all the people?

"A few days later, after quite a storm, we went back to that ship to salvage what we could. She was washed up farther onto the shore. The vessel was almost all out of the water by then. Rolling it onto its port side, we could see the underbelly of the ship. A huge chunk of the hull was missing; nearly a quarter of its length was gone. What was queer was that the planks were not ragged as you might expect. Instead it was something we'd seen a few times before. The planks were clean cut, almost as if they'd been sawed at some sawmill. Here's the thing, friends. It was shaped like a circle, kind of how an apple looks when you take a big bite right out of the middle."

Daniel stopped his narration. Even though they were all seated, some of the men were breathing heavily.

"That's what we saw. Ain't it, fellas?" Daniel asked.

To a person, every man around the room nodded but didn't speak a word.

Long Hands, sitting in the corner, broke the silence. "Katch Uneh."

14

THE HERMIT

ABOUT TWO MILES to the east of Little Cove, there was an island the locals called "Mound"—not "the Mound," not "Mound Island," just Mound.

Although there were many islands in the great lake, this was the closest to Little Cove. It was natural for the locals to reason through how Mound got where it was. When the great sea monster took a bite from the shore, which created Little Cove, it began to swim back into deeper waters. It took the sea monster a little time to realize that the sand and shore were not very tasty. So it spit out the contents into the lake, and that's how Mound got its start.

Mound became completely covered with trees in a wide variety of woods. Many animals and birds lived on Mound. It seemed to sustain itself. But the fishermen of Little Cove didn't visit Mound at all. There was no need.

However, it was helpful to be on the lee side of the island when winds were strong. If the wind was coming in from the west, the east side of the island would be the place to fish, as it would be protected. When a strong north wind blew in, the fishermen would go to the south side. That being said, Mound was just one of many areas to fish around the great lake.

One day, a fella rowed into Little Cove and pulled his boat onto the shore.

"Howdy, stranger."

"Howdy to you."

"Can we help you at all?"

"I hope you can. I need some supplies and tools. I've got money to pay."

Little Cove had grown enough that it had a small general store. The reliance upon vessels heading west and trading with the village was not the best way to get what the village needed. The store sold basic hand tools, fishing supplies, boat repair equipment, seeds, jugs, shoes, and even wood stoves.

"Can you point me where to go?"

"Just up the hill, that way to the right, and left at a big pine tree. Can't miss it."

That was the last they saw of the visitor. He apparently filled his rowboat with his supplies and off he went. No one got a name. No one knew where he came from or where he was heading.

That happened in the spring of the year. Nobody saw this man until the fall of the same year when he again arrived in his rowboat. He saw some children playing down by the water's edge. He went over and did a little jig for them. They giggled and clapped their hands. The children seemed to be enjoying themselves as much as the man was enjoying himself. But he didn't say much. He walked up to the general store and lugged his supplies back down to his boat. Then off he went as fast as a snap.

Of course, there was scuttlebutt all through the village and around the card tables at Bertha's Tavern.

"Who has seen that fella, comes here in a rowboat, then goes?"

Festus, Enis, and Zack said they had. The couple who owned the general store, Byron and Mary Waterman, of course, said they had.

"What did you learn about this fella, anyways?" they asked the Watermans.

"He was very private. He didn't say much. When we asked his name, he just said he wasn't given one. He had a list of supplies written down on a paper. We got them all. He paid for them. That was that."

"Anybody seen him up or down the shoreline?"

They all shook their heads "no."

With not much to go on, the conversation didn't last long.

A year or more passed, and he showed up again. Same thing. He bought supplies, and then he was gone. It was always a surprise when he showed up. The folks in Little Cove weren't ready for him with their questions.

"Next time he comes, I'm going ask him where he lives and where he goes when he leaves Little Cove. I know it's forward, not a very courteous thing, but I think we've a right to know."

"Back again, mister."

"That I am."

"Well, we here in Little Cove figure we got the right to ask where you live around these parts."

"I suspect you have."

After some silence, someone asked, "Well, where do you live? Where do you call home?"

He looked out at the great lake and simply said, "Out there."

It was clear; that was the way it was going to be.

The years rolled along. The man who came to be known as "the hermit" arrived every six months or thereabouts. He came for supplies and left, never speaking more than a few words.

Some of the fishermen remarked that they thought they saw smoke wafting up from the treetops on Mound, but there was no need to explore.

It could have been mist or fog or even a hatch of gnats. But there were always some more curious than the others. T. J. and Shorty sailed out one night with the sole intention of finding out what was going on. They pulled their boat onto the shore and started walking a deer trail toward the center of the island. There it was: a cabin in the woods. They could see a lantern and a couple of candles lighting up the inside. There they saw him, the hermit. They slipped away into the darkness and sailed back to Little Cove with the news.

"Well, if he don't want us to know where he lives, why should we care to know?"

"We know now."

"Does it make a difference?"

"It's his life; he can do what he wants."

"Sure he can, but now we know."

"I hope you won't be throwing it into his face the next time he rows in for supplies."

Six months came and went. A year came and went. A year and a half came and went. Everyone wondered. It was far past the time for the hermit to show up. He must have needed supplies, but there was no sign of him.

"Get on out there and see what's going on. You go, Shorty and T. J. You're the ones who were so curious."

They sailed out, walked up to the cabin, but saw no light. They knocked loudly on the door, but there was no answer. They walked in and looked around. There he was lying in his bed, all shriveled up, rotting. They went outside and started to dig a grave. They lowered him down. They shoveled on the dirt quickly.

"Oh Gawd, what stank!"

"Isn't his fault."

"Should we put a cross above?"

"No bother. Won't do him no good."

"Rest in peace, whoever you are."

Shorty and T. J. went back inside to look around a bit. It wasn't their lot to do anything with what little there was in the cabin. But they were both drawn to a box on the table. They opened it and found a letter.

"Should we read it?"

"I don't know, but I do know this. We're not taking any-thing from this cabin. If there's money, it's his, not ours. Nothing here is ours to take. He wanted to be alone. That was his choice. Everything that was his should stay. Even the con-tents of this letter we're about to read. There's not to be a word about any of this to the folks in Little Cove. We found the her-mit dead, buried him, and that was that. Are you agreed?"

"I agree, Shorty. Not a word. There's nothing needs be said. You're the better with reading. You go ahead. Read it, and then we'll put it back in the box and leave."

> My dear son,
>
> Your loving mother and I think about you daily. We wonder where you have gone. You left without a word. We have asked everyone we have met to look for you, and if they find you, to return you to our care.
>
> I have made many mistakes. I am sorrowfully smitten.
>
> I have prayed for forgiveness. I fear I will die with-out absolution. I have forgiven you, though I bear the scar on my neck.
>
> Your bothers, William, Robert, and Duff, send you their prayers.
>
> Your mother, Jessie, and I, your loving father, pray you will come home to us soon.
>
> Your father,
> Gavin MacLeod

"The hermit had a name, T. J."

"He surely did. May God have mercy on your soul, forgiv-ing your sins. Rest in peace, Bruce MacLeod."

15

"THERE'S NOWT SO QUEER AS FOLKS"—WELSH SAYING

ONE MIGHT THINK that today Little Cove must look and be very different from how it was centuries ago. The village must certainly be larger. The people there must have been carried along with the tide into the modern age. Little Cove must have grown, developed. Not so. Indeed, it may be one of those places that time forgot. It may be one of those last bastions of how it used to be.

Oh, yes, the interstate highway was built some miles to the south, running east to west. But it may as well be a hundred miles to the south. Today, everybody quickly drives by and few stop. In fact, Little Cove received more visitors in the early days than now. There's a railroad line that stretches all the way across the country. It's just a few miles to the south as well. But the goods and people just hurry on by. No train people stop at Little Cove. They never did. They don't today.

The stone lighthouse still stands though the gas-fueled lamp went out years ago. The lighthouse keeper's house has been trashed. The doors are always open. All the windows are broken. It's full of beer bottles, girls' panties, and candy bar wrappers.

The shell of the icehouse still stands, mostly used for boat storage now. The foundation of Bertha's Tavern, with that huge stone cellar to house barrels of whiskey and beer, is still there.

A new diner sprang up down the lane, mostly serving deep-fried perch and fries. The locals eat there. Just like in olden days, they're surprised to see a stranger come through the door.

There are still thirty to forty boats tied to rickety docks, but most of the old fishing boats have been replaced by sailboats and runabouts. It's still a poor village. The boats today are beat up and need painting, and they are nothing to crow about.

The homes still look raggedy, with asbestos shingles and tar- papered sides. Dirt paths still connect the homes. Cars are parked on lawns. There are still fishermen. The outer break wall remains, for now. The shape of the harbor is mostly as it was. It still looks like a great sea monster took a huge bite out of the shore.

The list of characters has changed, but in a sense they are still the same gathering of smelly fishermen, scallywags, drunks, and liars as in olden days.

There's Ronnie, who says he fell from a ladder. He claims he received a big settlement, so he bought his new boat, *Fish On*. Most believe he just got lucky at the new Indian casino a few hours' drive away.

There's Chester, who spent seven years building a Viking sailboat in his backyard. It was what they call a "double bow," pointed at both ends. It was a two-master. Chester launched it, sailed it once, and then he died.

There's still a Trapper, no relation to the Trapper of old. We think the name was just available so he took it. He's got a knack for catching lake perch like nobody else can. "Ah, my sweet perch," he croons.

Dave the doctor is a different kind. He blows into Little Cove each summer. He drops his boat into the water, sails away, comes back in a week, and puts the boat back on land. Then he disappears until the next year.

Renny Bartle? Well, Renny, he has two strikes against him. It's bad enough to be a drunk, but to be totally crazy too! He mostly looks like he put both hands into an electrical socket. About eleven months of the year he lives on his old sailboat, which is always on land. When it gets real cold, he takes a small room in town.

You'll recognize the next fella instantly: Larry the nudist. He has no religious or philosophical persuasion that compels him to be a nudist. He just likes to go around naked. He's a wrinkly old fella and hasn't got much to brag about anymore— or show off, for that matter. You'll often find him reading a book in a lawn chair under the shade of a tree. He will be buck naked.

Tommy runs a dive boat. It's no surprise that hundreds of ships lie on the bottom of the great lake. Tommy has re-searched a GPS location for many of them. Because those axes are his little secret, he does a fair business, taking out visiting divers who want to see particular vessels. He's probably the only "success story" there is.

A fella named Champion is the son of the man who operates the local marina. Champion is Ed's only son and a ne'er-do-well, a huge disappointment to his father. Champion spends most of his days throwing sticks into the lake for his black labs to retrieve. The marina has a building that leans this way and that. But if you're looking for a certain stainless screw or some other hardware, Ed will find it—if you have a few days.

There are a few dozen loners, fellas and gals, who stick to their boats, fixin' and fussin' and generally messin' around. Nobody asks them for much. They've nothing much to say.

Some of the old buildings were connected to create an an-tique shop. You'll find just about anything nautical you want from wheels and anchors to floats and boats. Too bad it's seldom open. Nobody can ever seem to track down the owner.

A couple artists hang about. One builds small lighthouses from shore stones, patterned after the Little Cove lighthouse. The other sets up his easel and paints ships upon the stormy sea, one after another after another. We think he might be clinically depressed.

There are a few chaps who gather around the tiki hut down by the shore. Storms destroyed a dozen or so shelters over the years. This is the last attempt for a gathering spot. As the sun goes down after hot August days, a few of the men and women still wander in with their Keystone Beer and apricot brandy, ready for communion before calling it a day. Sometimes there's a cookout. Visitors are generally welcome unless they don't look like one of us.

What about me? Most days you'll find me in a lawn chair sitting on the old wooden dock. I just pass the time and watch it all go by, too broken up to do much physically. I gaze at the schools of minnows swimming by, the endless display of clouds drifting on. I think about all those I've known who now only live in memory. If you can find your way to Little Cove—'tain't easy, you know—stop by and set a spell. I'll have a few more yarns to spin, and it'll be grand to hear yours.